Baked In Love

A NOVELLA

J.E. Smith

an imprint of Nicole Frail Books, LLC
Avoca, Pennsylvania

*To those who know the weight of loss but are brave
enough to believe in love anyways.*

"Maybe one day we'll find that place where you and I could be together. And we'll catch our dreams within the waves of change. So smile for me one last time and believe that we'll meet again. Until then, I'll be missing you."

—R.M. Drake

CHAPTER 1

Katie

*You're invited to join us to celebrate the marriage of
Julia Nash & Jacob White
on Friday, March 21, 2025,
at The Lakes Country Club.
In lieu of gifts, the bride and groom
are asking for donations to the
American Liver Cancer Institute
in honor of Julia's brother, Jeff,
who was a shining light of joy and optimism.*

I STARE AT MY YOUNGER sister's wedding invitation as I wait for my turn to exit the plane. I swore I would never come back to my hometown of Lakes, Arizona, but I can't abandon my sister on the most important day of her life. Especially since my brother isn't here to be part of it.

Julia had just graduated high school, and I was wrapping up an internship with Pascal Mirao, the best baker and cake decorator in Arizona, when Jeff had taken a turn for the worse.

After his death, I tucked tail and ran away to Hudsonville, Michigan, swearing never to return home, to the place that reminded me of him.

Stepping foot in my hometown will inevitably bring unwelcome memories and feelings to the surface, but there's one person I really hope to avoid: Travis Hardy. My brother's best friend and the one man I always wanted but could never have. I don't think I can face him, even after all these years.

"Finally, our turn," the lady in the seat mutters next to me, dragging me from my thoughts.

I pull my long, blonde hair into a ponytail and fix my glasses before standing to deplane.

The wedding is only two days away, and I am booked to fly back to Michigan the day after. From what I understand, the itinerary is simple: Today, family brunch. Tomorrow, rehearsal dinner. Friday, wedding. Saturday, I'm out of here.

As I walk through the airport, I spot my younger sister bouncing and waving as soon as she sees me. When I am off the escalator, she wraps me in the tightest hug. As much as I hate coming back here, it's incredible to see her again.

"Oh, Katie! It's so good to see you." Her voice, so

full of joy, warms me as she holds me tight. "I've missed you so much!"

"I've missed you, too, Jules," I say with a smile as she finally releases me. I fill my voice with enthusiasm that I don't really feel, simply because she deserves to hear it. "So . . . are you ready for the wedding festivities to begin?"

"Yes!" she squeals but then turns all business, like a switch has flipped in her. "Speaking of which, we have to go or we won't be able to pick up the pastries and coffee bar stuff from the bakery before the family brunch!"

In an instant, she turns and drags me through the airport toward her small, white car. I throw my bags into her trunk and climb in next to her. I'm barely buckled when she peels out faster than I feel is necessary.

It's only a fifteen-minute drive to the small town of Lakes, but my sister is driving like the world will end if we get even one minute off schedule. I never pegged Jules to be the Bridezilla type. She has always had a go-with-the-flow and carefree attitude about life, but I guess when it's the biggest day of your life, you're allowed to go a little crazy.

"So, anything new happening with you? It's been almost a month since we last had a real conversation." She whips the car around a rickety, old truck on the highway.

"Nope, same old boring me." I shrug.

I wish I had something exciting to share with her, but the truth is I've just been going through the motions of day-to-day life for a while now.

Her face falls slightly at my response, and she rockets past another car.

"Goodness, Jules. You can slow down a little bit." My stomach rolls, and I grip the grab handle above the passenger-side window for some stability. "We'll make it. Everything will be okay."

"Sorry, I just can't have *anything* go wrong. I love Jacob and just want everything to be perfect. You'll understand when it's you some day."

"Yeah, maybe someday." I smile at her, but I doubt it's in my future anytime soon.

She takes the off ramp and drives us straight into our hometown. Lakes is the same as I remember. All the stores are on the main road through town, with the church at the end before the road climbs the small mountain. The townsfolk are walking around carrying various bags and totes, and I recognize everyone. One perk of small-town living—or downfall, depending on who you ask.

Jules pulls up in front of the bakery, which has received both a makeover and a name change since I left. Butter Your Buns Bakery is a small shop with two tables out front and a huge glass window showing the modern interior with blue and gray tones throughout.

"Oh crap, I forgot to call the caterer with the setup time

for the rehearsal dinner!" Jules scowls at her phone. "Katie, can you go in and grab the stuff while I handle this?" She looks up at me, ready to beg.

"Really? Can't you call the caterer later?" I drone, not wanting to leave the car and risk running into anyone. Chances are too high I'll get sucked into a conversation I don't want to have.

"No, I don't want to forget again. It's just a few things, please?" She gives me her best pleading expression—big eyes, pouty mouth, and all—something she's perfected as the baby of the family.

My heart clenches as my eyes shift back to the bakery. Travis's mom used to own it, and we all spent a lot of time here. When things were hard, Jeff and I would come here to work out our problems over coffee and sweets.

That's the problem with being here: his memory is painted everywhere.

"I guess if I must," I concede to her, simply because that's what Jeff would have done for me. She deserves the same older-sibling love.

"Thank you! You're the best! The order is under my name and should already be paid for." A bright smile spreads across her face and she immediately pulls up the caterer's number.

I climb out of the car and make my way into the cute little bakery where people are eating and drinking coffees at tiny tables throughout. As I approach the counter, my stomach sinks and I freeze in my tracks.

Travis is working the coffee counter and register.

The first person I have to communicate with in Lakes is the last person I wanted to see in town.

I don't need more than a few seconds to see that, over the past five years, he has managed to become even better looking than I remember. He has gone from tall and lean to somehow possessing muscles that now strain his T-shirt. Tattoos cover his left arm, and his once short, chocolate-brown hair has grown out and is tied up in a sexy manbun.

The last time I saw him flashes through my mind like the unwelcome memory it is.

I was hiding in the back room of the funeral home, trying my best to avoid the sympathetic gazes of all those who knew Jeff.

I was sick of hearing how great Jeff was, how he would be dearly missed, that he'd had such a bright future.

Silent tears streamed down my cheeks, but I couldn't cry out like I wanted to. I couldn't let everyone hear me.

A knock sounded on the door, and I looked over my shoulder to see Travis slipping in.

He walked up behind me, close enough that we were almost touching.

"Are you okay?" His voice cracked as he spoke, like he was on the verge of tears, too.

"Fine. I just needed a minute before the service." I stuffed all the hurt back inside my cracked heart and batted away the last of my tears.

"You don't need to pretend with me. I'm here, Katie. I'll always be here."

My heart yearned for him. I wanted to cry into his chest and feel his arms tighten around me as I release all my pain and grief. But I couldn't. Not with Travis.

"I said I'm fine. Thank you for the concern."

I turned for the door and walked out the room.

That day I shut the door on so much more than my concerned friend, and now I have to face him.

Steeling myself, I approach as he builds a latte on the back counter. "Be with you in a moment," he tosses over his shoulder.

He turns around and pauses as he looks over my face, and I swallow hard as butterflies erupt in my belly.

"Becky, here is your latte," he shouts without taking his eyes off me, and I can only stand frozen. "It's been a long time, Katie." His voice is flat and monotonous.

"Yeah, it has."

Why is this so awkward? He was constantly around growing up, but I haven't talked to him since the funeral. He called and texted me multiple times, but I didn't want to talk to him, because it meant remembering my brother was gone. I pushed Travis away, just like I had everyone else.

"You're in town for the wedding?" he asks.

"Yeah, that's why I'm here. I need to pick up Jules's order."

"Sure thing." He smiles at me like I'm just another customer to please, and I hate it. "Max, can you get Julia Nash's order from the back and carry it to her car? It's the white Chevy out there."

"Absolutely," Max yells back from behind the kitchen door. Travis turns to me now and punches a few keys on the register.

"I thought you were working construction with your dad. Why are you in the bakery?" I ask, unable to resist my curiosity.

"Dad retired and I decided to take over this place from my mom instead. I didn't want to work construction without Jeff by my side."

"Oh . . . I guess that's understandable." I shift on my feet, feeling uncomfortable.

"What have you been doing with yourself up in Michigan?"

"I work as a freelance cake decorator for various bakeries. It's fun. Pays the bills." I shrug.

"That seems like a good fit for you." He looks up from the register, and I feel heat flood my cheeks as his eyes lock on to mine. I still feel like the high school girl who was head over heels for him, except now I'm twenty-five and a grown adult! Goodness, I need to get a grip on myself.

Someone clears their throat behind me, and I realize I'm holding up a line that has now formed.

"Oh, my bad. I guess I better go, or Jules will start freaking out about being late." I laugh awkwardly and turn for the door, walking away.

"Katie!" he shouts, and I turn to look at him. "You um . . . you look great."

I nod and smile, feeling my blush deepen as I head out the door to the car.

CHAPTER 2

Katie

"SERIOUSLY, JULES, YOU COULD HAVE given me a heads-up that Travis owned the bakery," I scold my sister as we continue to set up brunch on my parents' back patio.

"I didn't think it was a big deal." She shrugs as she arranges the muffins on a platter. "He's been around forever and still helps us with bigger things that need to be done."

"I was just shocked to see him is all." I try my best to sound nonchalant, but inside I'm screaming.

He was the only person I had wanted to totally and completely avoid on this trip home.

All it took was one look into his honey-colored eyes

and a single smile for the feelings I had locked away in a deep part of me to rush back to the surface.

"Well, you should get used to it, because he's one of Jacob's groomsmen *and* making the wedding cake."

Of course he is.

It wouldn't feel like home if I wasn't drooling over my brother's best friend.

I take a deep breath and carry the plates to the table.

It's only three days and then you won't have to talk to or see him. You can do this.

Jacob and his parents are the first to arrive, and Jules basically jumps into his arms when she spots him. She has been infatuated with him since the day they met, and I wonder if, five years from now, she will still be leaping into his embrace when he enters a room.

I smile at the sight of them as I continue the last of the setup. It's sweet to see her so in love, and she deserves her happy ending.

My love life is a mess, so at least one of us has it figured out.

I've dated off and on since moving to Michigan, but in the end, I called them all off because I couldn't shake the feeling that they would never win my brother's approval. They were always tools with self-inflated egos and horrible red flags or so soft that I would have to take care of them. No, only one man would have ever had a shot at winning my brother's approval.

But it's not possible. We can't be together.

Other guests begin to arrive, and I am berated with the never-ending questions. Just when I am ready to shout, *Yes, I'm single, and I don't plan to move home!* to the third aunt who asks, I excuse myself and go to the coffee bar. Coffee always makes everything better— even family members who are a bit too nosy become more tolerable.

I pour myself a cup, add way too much cream, and top it with a chocolate drizzle. Today calls for some extra sugar.

I close my eyes and lean forward on the coffee bar, inhaling the warmth of my beverage. I survived the bakery this morning, and I'll survive all the family questioning, too.

"Ahem." A deep, smooth voice clears their throat, and I jump and whip around.

Travis is here.

"I'd like to get some coffee, too, if you don't mind."

Why did we have to stop at the bakery if he was coming anyway? "Umm, why are you here?" I whisper with an aggravated bite.

He raises his eyebrows at me and crosses his huge arms like I have offended him. "Because I was invited."

"Today is for family only. You're not family."

A smirk plasters his face, and he wets his bottom lip, making all my focus go to his perfect mouth. The old desire to kiss him resurfaces.

I bite my bottom lip slightly and redirect my focus

back to my frustration; it's all I have to ground me with him so close.

"Travis *is* family!" My dad comes up behind him and slaps a hand on his shoulder. "He basically lived here when he and your brother were in high school."

I roll my eyes, and Travis wears a smug grin.

"Dad, we need you over here for some pictures!" Jules yells as she waves at him.

"Excuse me, Katie-Bear. I'll be back soon." He leans over, kisses my cheek, and whisks off to attend to the demanding bride-to-be.

"Aww, it's sweet your dad still calls you Katie-Bear," Travis teases as he fills a cup of coffee. "Though I much prefer Gummy Bear."

I whirl to fully face him at the sound of the old nickname he and my brother used to tease me with. He doesn't get to use that anymore. Not without Jeff.

I seethe at him, grab my coffee, and start toward my seat.

"Screw you, Travis!" I throw over my shoulder.

"Bet you wish you could!" he yells after me, and I know his perverse joke has me turning redder than a cherry, especially since there's an edge of truth to it.

As I take my seat, I notice all the eyes on me. Over half the party probably heard that exchange between us, and thankfully there is no pyre, because this place would burst into flames from the level of my embarrassment.

As everyone resumes their conversations, my father takes a seat in the chair next to me.

"Are you okay, Katie-Bear? That looked . . . intense." He glances toward the coffee station and then back to me.

"Yeah, just a misunderstanding, Dad." I place my hand on his arm, trying to reassure him. Dad cares with his whole heart, and I can't have him pressing me. Jules's wedding weekend can't become about *my* messy life.

"Okay, as long as you're sure? I don't mind having a word with Travis." His voice is stern, and he raises an eyebrow at me.

I roll my eyes as I smile at my overprotective father. "Yes, I'm sure."

As soon as the words leave my mouth, Jules stands, clanking her mimosa glass with a fork.

"Thank you all for coming. Everything is set up and ready for us to enjoy some food. Let's eat, and then we can cover details for the upcoming events."

She smiles at all of us and then turns to Jacob, who wraps his arm around her waist and looks down at her with nothing but love.

"Alright, let's get some food. But sweetheart, know I'm always here for you no matter what." Dad stands from his chair and kisses my forehead.

"I know, Dad."

I nod at him with a smile, but my heart pangs. Dad is always here for us girls, but over the past five years, I've kept everyone at arm's length, including him.

Dad leaves me and heads to the coffee bar, and I move to the food line, but the emotions of the day have stolen most of my appetite.

Luckily, the rest of brunch moves forward without a hiccup, and we're able to celebrate Jules and Jacob as a family. They run each of us through the event schedules, and Jules is excited, to say the least, but she is also stressed beyond measure. I'm worried about her; a stroke would be less than ideal while trying to keep everything perfect and on time.

After the last of the extended family has left, the tedious task of the afterparty cleanup begins.

I carry the leftover muffins into the house and notice Jules is in the kitchen micromanaging Travis. I decide to stay hidden just on the other side of the wall and experience a certain sense of pleasure overhearing their exchange.

"Okay, so the cake and cupcakes are done and the desserts for the reception will be ready for tomorrow?" Jules inquires.

"Yes. Trust me, Julia, I have everything under control on my end. Relax and try to enjoy this. You only get married once." He soothes her with a comforting voice that makes my butterflies erupt again.

Why the hell does he have to be so sweet? It makes being upset with him difficult.

"TRAVIS!" Jacob's panicked voice fills the house as he blows in off the porch.

Crap, hopefully he didn't notice me eavesdropping.

"Dispatch just called me in. There's a fire at the bakery!"

CHAPTER 3

Travis

THE BAKERY IS MY WHOLE life. I've poured every ounce of blood, sweat, and tears into this place and even built an apartment above it where I live.

And I watched as it burned.

The last of the fire is out now, and the firefighters are starting to clean up, but I just stand, frozen, staring at the rubble of my life.

Anything of real importance in my life always seems to leave. First, Jeff.

Even after he got sick, I never wanted to imagine he would leave me, but he did, and I miss him daily.

Then, Katie. She was my closest friend after Jeff. I told Katie everything, and her carefree spirit was a joy to be in the presence of. As we got older, I often found myself wishing I could hold her close, kiss her perfect pink lips and make her mine, but that was never going to happen because Jeff was my best friend. And then she up and moved to Michigan without even so much as a goodbye text. A piece of me died with Jeff, and after Katie left, I've never been quite whole.

Now the sanctuary I created is in shambles, too.

What the hell do I do now?

I don't even have a place to sleep tonight. My parents sold the family house and are currently traveling the country in an RV, so going home isn't a possibility anymore, either.

"Oh, Travis, I'm so sorry!" Mrs. Nash approaches and wraps me in her warm embrace.

She has always been like a second mom to me.

Looking behind her, I see the whole crew came with her. Julia is talking to Jacob, Mr. Nash is scowling at the bakery like he's as upset as I am, and Katie is staring right at me.

I wish hers were the arms wrapped around me right now.

She has no idea how much I've missed her over the years. Jeff made it more than clear she was off-limits in high school, and I respected his boundaries because that's what you do for a person who's more like a brother than a friend, but I can't help but wonder what would've happened if I hadn't.

Maybe Katie would have never left town.

Maybe she would be mine.

Mrs. Nash releases me and takes my face in her hands. "Tell me what you need."

"I don't even know where to begin. My apartment above the bakery needs repairs, along with part of the kitchen. On top of that, all the food that was prepped for the wedding has to be thrown out due to smoke damage."

I place my hands on my hips in exacerbation.

"Oh, sweet boy, I know this is a big hit for you, but let us help you." Her voice is desperate, and her eyes well with tears. "You can come stay in the guesthouse with Katie. There's an extra bedroom and a huge kitchen that you can work out of for now."

"What? Mom, no! Why can't he stay in Jeff's old room or something?" Katie chimes in from behind her mother, clearly annoyed.

I knew after Jeff died that everything changed between us, but for her to want to avoid my company completely is ridiculous.

"Jeff's room is Jeff's room, Katie." Her mom pins her eyes on her and her voice holds a warning tone. "He can stay in the guesthouse with you."

My first thought is to decline, but with Katie's reaction, I can't pass up an opportunity to get under her skin even more. I want to work this out with her, but if she won't let me, then she leaves me no choice. She's ignored every attempt I've made to try and connect with her, to be there for her, but now that she's back, I won't let her get away again so easily.

"Thank you for the offer. Staying at the guesthouse would be a huge help, plus the kitchen is big enough for me to remake the cake." I smile at Katie the whole time I speak, and her little attitude is on full display with a silent scoff and her arms folded over her chest.

Oh, this is going to be so much fun.

"Perfect!" Her mom claps her hands together. "It's settled then. I still have all of Katie's old baking equipment from her internship, as well. So, just come over whenever you're ready."

"Will do. Thank you again."

"Of course, dear, that's what family is for." She smiles at me and heads off to go talk to her husband, leaving me alone with a thoroughly irritated Katie.

"What's wrong, Gummy Bear? Can't handle sharing a house for the next few days?"

"Stop with the Gummy Bear thing!" she shouts, moving toward me and stepping into my space.

"Sorry." I hold up my hands in surrender. "I just love seeing you look like a tiny Hulk with all that pent-up rage, when we both know you're just so sweet and soft." I lower my face next to her ear, and I don't miss her breath hitching as I do. Keeping my voice at a whisper, I add, "Like a gummy bear."

She shoves me back, but I don't budge.

"You're a real jerk, you know that?" she yells at me.

"I cannot wait to get out of this town and away from *you*!"

She turns on her heels and walks away, her hips swaying.

Oh, I am definitely under her skin, and I can't wait to push her until she cracks. We both know that she's shoving me away on purpose, but if her shaky breathing is any indication, there's something more going on here than just hatred for me.

"Travis, a word, please." Mr. Nash approaches me and claps his hand on my shoulder.

"Yes, sir?" I'm almost confident I know what this is about.

"You mind explaining what's going on between you and my daughter? That's the second time today that she's walked away from you upset."

I smile at the man who has looked out for me for as long as I can remember.

"I wish I could, but to be honest, I'm not really sure myself." I look back to the broken bakery. "She's a mystery to me, but I can't leave her alone."

I pause, but Mr. Nash only waits for me to continue.

"She left me here without even an explanation, then has ignored me ever since. I can't let her leave town again without trying to repair our friendship."

I sigh at the omission.

Everyone knows how difficult it was for me after

losing Jeff and then Katie. Hell, I almost lost myself, but Mr. Nash and Jacob made sure I didn't.

"I can understand that. Katie has always been one with a short fuse, but just be careful. It's not easy for her to be back here, and I don't want her to be gone permanently. She's my daughter, and I can't have you hurt her, Travis."

I turn to meet his gaze. I would never purposely cause Katie any harm. I don't think my own heart would allow it.

"I won't hurt her. You have my word."

He nods at me. "I'll hold you to that." He claps my shoulder twice and walks away.

This is a mess, to say the least, but I won't break my word. Katie won't be hurt, not on my account at least.

No, the only real heart on the line is mine. Katie has been my friend forever, but deep down, I know she is so much more than that.

CHAPTER 4

Katie

TWO DAYS. ONLY TWO MORE days, and then I can go back to Michigan and leave everything in this tiny town behind, including him.

Deep breaths, Katie. Deep breaths.

Last night was a complete mess. He kept walking around this tiny house like he owns it!

I haven't had any relief in the annoyance I feel toward him, and I'm about ready to kill him. It's seven in the morning, and he's running the huge stand mixer in the kitchen! How can anyone sleep through that?

I groan into my pillow and, in a fit of fury, I climb out of bed, throw on my red, glittery slippers, and stomp my way to the kitchen.

He is completely oblivious to my arrival. The mixer

is turning, and he's looking at a recipe card while sipping a cup of coffee like this is his everyday routine.

"SERIOUSLY, TRAVIS!" I yell over the mixer, getting his attention.

He moves to the machine and shuts it off. Then he meets my gaze, a smug smirk on his face. God, how I would love to knock it right off.

"It's seven in the morning! Some people actually like to sleep, you know." I cross my arms over my chest.

He sighs before setting down his coffee and walking over to stand in front of me. His eyes trail down my body and then back up.

Seriously, is he checking me out right now?

I roll my eyes in annoyance.

"I couldn't sleep last night, and some of us have work to do. I have to have the cake made by this afternoon so my decorator can come this evening because he can't come tomorrow." He places a hand on his hip and sighs. "I would do it myself, but most of my supplies were destroyed last night."

Guilt pangs in my chest at my lack of empathy, and I take a minute to really look at him.

He looks like hell. His eyes have dark circles beneath them and they're slightly puffy and red. The normal light energy he carries is still there, but it's almost like it's been doused in water.

I soften toward him and sigh. "Just give me until nine, noise-free, and I'll decorate the cake, okay?"

He wets his bottom lip, and his eyes search mine, contemplating my offer. "All right, you've got yourself a deal."

I wonder how those lips would feel on mine.

Stuffing the thought down, I give him a victorious smile. "Thank you!" I turn toward my room, ready for more sleep.

"No problem. Nice messy bun and slippers, by the way. It's a good look for you," he teases, but I'm too tired to play his games right now, so I slam my bedroom door closed in response.

I'm woken by the blaring noise of the mixer once more. Groaning, I look at my phone. Nine on the dot. *Well, no one will ever say he's late*, I sneer to myself.

Tonight is the rehearsal dinner, and Jules is probably an anxious mess. I need to head up to the big house to make sure she doesn't need anything extra from me. At the very least, I want to give her a hug and assure her that her wedding will be perfect. My poor mother doesn't need to be dealing with Bridezilla all alone this morning, especially now that Travis has to remake all the baked goods.

I hop in the shower and then dress in my favorite Red Wings hockey T-shirt and skinny jeans—the pair that make my butt look amazing—before heading to the kitchen. I need the extra confidence boost today. On the inside, I feel like a messed-up cupcake that's been dropped on the floor, but on the outside, I want to be the one with the perfect swirl of icing covered in shiny sprinkles.

When I arrive in the kitchen, Travis has continued his work. He pauses before adding ingredients to a bowl and stares at me with a twinkle in his eye. Or maybe I'm wishing there's a twinkle there. Either way, under his gaze, my pulse quickens, and butterflies erupt in my stomach.

I shove down the unwelcome feelings.

"I'm going up to the big house. Let me know when you're ready for me to decorate."

"Okay, tell everyone I said hi."

He nods and takes a sip from his coffee mug. I wonder if the man drinks coffee all day. It's the only thing I've actually seen him drink since I've been home, and I've now been back in Lakes almost twenty-four hours.

Shoes on, I hurry out the front door and come face-to-face with Jules.

"Well, good morning." She eyes me curiously. "What has you rushing out the door so fast?"

"Oh, nothing, just coming to see if you needed anything for tonight."

I start walking toward the main house at a pace that forces my sister to nearly chase after me.

"Oh, nothing? Right. So, you scurrying out of there had nothing to do with your new housemate?" she eagerly asks.

"What? No. If anything, he's annoying to have around!"

She jogs in front of me, making me stop, and raises her eyebrows at me.

"Katie, I know when you're holding back, and you're definitely holding back! Did something happen between you two that I don't know about?"

I feel my cheeks heat at her words. Why does my body always betray me?

"Nothing happened. He's Jeff's best friend and that's that."

"Yeah, and you're blushing. Do you have feelings for him?"

"Really, Jules?" I whine, begging her to drop something for once in her life.

"Ha! You do! How did I not know about this?" She throws her hands on her hips like she has been wronged in some way.

"Okay, we're done here. We're not going to talk about any feelings I may or may not have for Travis. Do *you* need anything?"

"Nope, I'm all set."

She gives me a knowing smile, and I narrow my eyes.

"Okay, well, goodbye then. I'll see you this evening."

I can feel my sister's eyes burn into the back of my head the whole way back to the guesthouse.

Once inside, I shut the door and lean on it, letting the relief of escaping my sister's questioning wash over me. Travis and I will never happen, and that is exactly why I keep those feelings strictly to myself.

I push off the door and start toward the living room.

"That was a fast visit." Travis's voice flutters in from the kitchen.

Of course he's spotted me. It must be written into this wedding weekend's agenda that I be forbidden to ever get a moment of peace!

I work up the best fake smile I can muster to hide the stress I feel.

"Yeah, they were set for the day. So, I'm going to chill here until setup this afternoon."

He walks in from the kitchen, wiping his hands on a towel.

"Actually, if you're free, would you be able to help me for a few? Julia really wanted strawberry heart thumbprint cookies for the dinner tonight, and if I remember right, yours were always the best." A soft smile graces his face as he speaks.

Is he flirting with me?

"They *are* the best. I make them for some local bakers here and there, and the townsfolk in Hudsonville always love them."

He laughs, and I smile at the sound.

"Wow, are you always so humble?" he jests, and I smack his chest playfully. He throws his hands up as if to block another attack. "And so violent?"

I laugh at his feigned injury and then sigh.

"All right, I guess I'll help."

I groan like I'm so inconvenienced, but really, the

idea of sharing the kitchen with him and having the opportunity to bake for my sister's wedding is enticing. "Now, move it! I've got cookies to make."

35

CHAPTER 5

Travis

SHE'S A BEAUTY TO WATCH in the kitchen. My four round cakes are in the oven now, so I'm just leaning against the wall and watching her magic unfold. She glides through the kitchen, adding various ingredients to different bowls, preparing the dry mixture, the wet, and the filling.

I remember watching her practice when she was doing her internship with Pascal Mirao. The kitchen was her happy place, where she always had this light and joyful energy. Her focus on the meticulous details, the pride she would exude when she had Jeff and I taste-test her newest creations. She has that light energy to her now, and I haven't seen it since before her brother died.

She belongs in the kitchen, baking and creating masterpieces. She's meant to be doing this.

I leave my place on the wall and walk up next to her, wanting to be a part of her magic and not simply observing it from the sideline. Lost in her own world, she turns and runs squarely into my chest, the small bowl of flour in her hands jostling enough for flour to fly everywhere, covering both of us.

"Oh, goodness!" she exclaims. "I didn't realize you were standing there."

"I gathered that." I gesture to my floured shirt. "It looked like you needed some help."

"I'm good actually." She turns back to the flour container to refill the bowl she had been taking to the mixer.

"No, Gummy Bear," I tease, following close behind her until I've trapped her against the counter. "You *do* need help. You're not nearly messy enough to call yourself a baker."

Before she knows what's happening, I gracefully scoop a handful of flour into my hand and drop it right on the top of her head. Then I immediately retreat.

"Ahh! Travis!" she squeals. "My hair!"

I take another step back, laughing at her powdered hair and face. She's biting her bottom lip in a suppressed giggle, and my chest warms at the sight.

She saunters over to me, a mischievous glint in her eyes. "You think this is funny, do you?"

"Oh, this is the funniest thing I've seen all week."

Quick as a whip, she swipes an egg off the counter and cracks it over my shoulder. Then she dashes for the corner of the kitchen and laughs at me. I look at my egg-soaked shirt and then back to her with a cunning smile.

"Sweetheart, you just started something you can't finish."

I playfully growl and dart toward her. I wrap one arm around her waist, and she squeals and thrashes as I drag her over to the counter. I grab the sugar—"You need some of *this*"—and laugh as I dump some on her.

She wiggles against my hold but manages to get the spoon from the jam jar. She smears it across my cheek. "Ha! Gotcha!"

I grab the bag of flour and drop it forcefully onto the counter, sending a white cloud into the air that sprinkles down on both of us. She turns to face me with a lightness to her that makes my heart stop. Both of our chests are heaving, and the laughter dies out.

"There, you're definitely a baker now," I say, holding her icy-blue eyes with mine. She bites her bottom lip, and longing pulls in my chest. She has always been more to me than just my best friend's sister, and now I don't want to hold back anymore. Jeff is gone, and we're adults. I can't say goodbye to her again without even trying.

She steps closer to me and tips her chin, daring me to

take what I want. Cupping her cheek, I slide my thumb over her lips, wiping away the flour remnants. Her eyes flutter at my touch and her lips part. She desires for me to kiss her just as much as I want to.

I lean down and kiss her pillow-soft lips. Every nerve ending lights up inside me as she deepens our kiss and laces her fingers in my hair.

Every doubt I ever had about what I have felt all these years disappeared as soon as her lips hit mine. This is what I've been wanting, needing. This is *right*. Katie is the missing piece in my life.

I lift her, and her legs wrap around my waist as I walk her to the counter. Our mouths never stop dancing.

Fire ignites in my veins, and the need to never let this woman go solidifies in me.

A knock on the door sounds, and she pulls away from me.

"Travis, the door."

"Forget them. We're busy right now." My voice is deep, husky. I don't want to leave this moment with her.

I lean in to kiss her again, but she places a hand on my chest, stopping me.

"Travis, we can't." She pauses and lets out a shaky breath. "This can never happen between us, and you know it. This was a mistake."

Her eyes fill with a deep sadness. The sight of it is a

knife to my chest. She slides from the counter and heads straight for the bathroom with barely a hesitation.

Irritation engulfs me. Jeff would have been upset with me and Katie if he were here today, but I know in time he would have approved. He would have known I would take care of her the way she deserves. But she's so stuck in what *she* thinks her brother would think to even give us a chance.

She called that life-altering kind of kiss a *mistake*.

Another knock sounds on the door, and I walk to it still covered in our baking mess.

I yank it open and find Jacob. His eyes scan me, and a knowing smirk forms. He's holding a stack of clothes I can only assume are meant for me.

"What the hell happened to you?"

"Nothing, just working on making the cake and dessert for dinner tonight."

I open the door, and he strides into the house, setting the clothes on the table.

"You know, I've been to the bakery many times while you were working, and I can't recall even once when you had more than a little flour on an apron." He sounds almost cocky about it, and I want to kick him out of this house.

"Shut up, man. Did you need something or are you just here to harass me?" I scowl at him.

The shower starts in the bathroom, catching Jacob's attention before he returns it to me.

"Were you baking with Katie?"

"Does it matter if I was?" I feel defensive, worried he's going to tell me to stay away—just like Jeff had.

"Yeah, it does!" he exclaims. "You two have been pining after each other forever. You're the only ones who never noticed, and maybe Jules, but she never picks up on those sorts of things." He laughs as he slaps me on the back.

There's no way he's right. If Katie had been interested in me all this time, she would never have pushed me away.

I scoff at the notion. "If she were interested in me all these years, Jeff would have said something. The only thing he ever told me was to leave her be or he would knock my teeth in."

"Why do you think he told you that, man? Probably because he knew she liked you and didn't want to see you break her heart. He would've had to break your kneecaps for that."

He crosses his arms and smiles at me like I'm an idiot. And maybe I am. . . .

"It's time you shoot your shot with her, Travis."

"I can't, okay? I just kissed her in the kitchen, and she shut me down because of Jeff. She's never going to be open to anything between us. I know her well enough to know that she would rather spend the rest of her life alone than dishonor any of her brother's wishes."

The words are bitter as I speak, but they're the truth and completely unavoidable.

"Look, my best advice is to go to the big house and get cleaned up. Take some time to think, and I know you'll figure this out." He winks at me as the timer for my cakes goes off. They'll need time to cool, so doing as he suggests is possible.

I move to the kitchen and pull out the cakes, setting them gently on the glass stovetop and on the counter with hot pads.

I guess cleaning up and taking time to think this through isn't a bad idea.

"You're probably right. Let me clean up here and then I'll take some time for me."

Lord knows that girl in there is stubborn and loyal to her core, so if I'm to get through to her, I'm going to need a miracle or something.

CHAPTER 6

Katie

DID HELL FREEZE OVER? OR did I miss the memo that the Lions actually made it to the Super Bowl?

Because Travis just kissed me.

And I know it was real because I'm still scrubbing the sugar from my scalp!

This cannot be happening right now. It's both my literal dream come true and my worst nightmare!

That kiss made my heart stutter and my body melt, made me feel alive. It made the whole blasted world stop turning.

For the first time since Jeff died, I felt . . . whole.

But it can't happen. None of this can happen.

I let the water wash over my face, hoping it will take some of these feelings with it.

Jeff was the only one who ever suspected my crush on Travis, and he told me never to go there. That Travis was his best friend and was a playboy to his core. Which . . . was true in high school. But not after Jeff got sick. Regardless, I'd promised him that he never had to worry, that I wouldn't. I gave him my word before he was ever sick, so how can I break that?

Travis may be a changed man, and if my brother were alive, maybe we could reason with him, but I can't betray him now that he's gone.

Ugh. Life sucks sometimes.

With the last of the sugar and flour washed away, I climb out of the shower and throw on my bathrobe. Exiting the bathroom, I figure Travis will still be in the kitchen, but he's gone, and the kitchen is clean.

Did he go to the big house?

Disappointment starts to creep in at the thought.

Nope, I'm shutting that down right now.

I am not his keeper, and I don't care whether he's here or not!

Maybe if I tell myself this enough, I'll start to believe it.

Once in my room, I dress in my favorite baggy sweatpants and a tight tank top. I need something to ground me, and comfy clothes help somewhat. I toss up my wet hair into a messy bun, not caring about how it will affect styling it for the party later.

Why did I come home? I can't say I was exactly happy

in Michigan, but at least there I didn't have all these lingering, complicated feelings demanding be addressed.

Kissing Travis was a mistake. Now, denying myself him will be even harder.

Why did I make that promise to my brother? Why did he have to go and die with it?

My head is reeling, but I won't let the pain swallow me whole. I can't. Instead, I shake my head and swallow that painful feeling, locking it behind the steel vault in my chest.

Now, I have cookies to make, along with a cake to decorate. I nod at my reflection in the bedroom mirror, resolved to focus on the tasks ahead.

I rip my bedroom door open and head to the living room, grab the small Bluetooth speaker, and make my way back to the kitchen.

With the house empty, it's time for a baking party. I connect my phone, blast my favorite Katy Perry playlist, and get to work.

A while later, the cookies are done and packed for dinner tonight. I'll have to do the cake this evening since Travis failed to come back and never told me what it's supposed to look like.

Abandoning the kitchen, I head to my room and change into my dress for the rehearsal dinner. It's dark green, form-fitting, and stops at my knees. Next, I slide on gray heels and then add some silver earrings. To finish off my look, I add some loose curls to my hair and light makeup. This evening will be great, and I will avoid Travis like the plague to my heart that he is.

With my small clutch in tow, I load up the car with the cookie boxes and climb in the driver's seat. I start the engine and peer in the rearview mirror. The main house is in perfect view, and my heart aches slightly. *He* is probably in there.

Hopefully Travis and I can just forget that kiss ever happened, for both our sakes. We're friends, and no matter how much I wish it could be different, it's never going to be.

I throw the car into gear and take off toward the country club to meet the caterer.

Two days. Two more days and I will leave him and this town behind to nurse my aching heart in Hudsonville, Michigan.

Again.

CHAPTER 7

Travis

MY SHOULDERS ARE TIGHT WITH tension that I can't seem to shake as the hot water beats my back. This shower was supposed to help clear my head, but I'm pretty sure it has only made it worse. All night, my mind replayed the fresh memories of the bakery in flames, on repeat, instead of allowing me to escape through just a few hours of sleep. And now, all day long, and especially since we kissed, it has decided I must be consumed by thoughts of Katie.

I'm just spiraling in here.

Katie is in the guesthouse locking away any feelings she ever had for me.

She's going to run again. I can feel it. But can I stop it?

This shouldn't be this difficult.

Kissing her felt so right. It sealed my fate—I now know I will never be able to let her go. If I could, I would punch Jeff right now for ever keeping us apart. But instead, I curse him beyond the grave. He left me here to deal with life alone, face every obstacle alone, to take care of *his* family. And to thank me for all that, to prepare me for this lonely existence, I can't even have the woman I've wanted forever because he took any chance of that with him.

I admit I was a stupid, immature, crappy guy back then—one who used women and then discarded them like they were nothing—but I would have never done that to Katie, and he had no way of knowing the man I would turn into. Hell, I didn't even know who I'd be, or who I even wanted to be back then, so how could he have known?

Sorrow and anger pangs in my chest. I miss my friend—my brother—but I'm still so mad that he left me here. I'm mad that he is keeping her from me.

I climb out of the worthless shower, quickly dry off, and throw on the T-shirt and basketball shorts that Jacob brought me. What the hell do I do now?

Women are strange creatures. My gut is screaming at me to go back to the guesthouse and work it out with her, but what if space is what she needs?

No, what she *needs* is her brother.

I swallow hard, knowing what I must do.

When Jeff died, he left us all letters. Final words of sorts. But Katie was never given hers because she took off before anyone found them. Her letter should still be in the nightstand next to Jeff's bed.

I walk the hallway until I'm standing in front of his white door. I've been in this room more times in my life than any other room in this house, but only twice since he passed. Nobody comes in here. Mrs. Nash has her cleaning lady clean it, because she can't come in here herself. None of us can, really. Jeff's death left us all with a hole in our lives that will never be filled.

I twist the knob and push the door open, revealing all the beautiful and painful memories within. His gray walls, covered in photos of all of us smiling and laughing. The whole family on the beach, Julia and Jacob in their football/cheerleading attire, Katie in a goofy selfie with her tongue stuck out, him and me at a rock concert. We were all so carefree, all so young.

His three guitars are on their stands in the corner, even though he could hardly play. He was convinced we would someday start a band together.

I eye the baseball magazine on his dresser that actually holds inappropriate photos of women. We thought we were so smart to disguise it like that.

My heart aches being in this room, but it's also where I feel my friend the most. God, I miss him. I miss the laughs, the advice, the sketchy crap we would get into, even the arguments. I would give so much for him to be here today. It's not fair he was taken from us so early.

I cross the room to the nightstand and pull open the drawer to reveal her letter still inside. I grab it, shut the drawer, and walk over to his dresser. This magazine should have been moved somewhere out of sight years ago, but I couldn't bring myself to touch it. It's only a matter of time before Mrs. Nash finds the contents, though, and what's inside should be a secret Jeff gets to keep even in death.

I chuckle to myself as I lift the magazine and look for a suitable spot to stash it.

The top shelf in the closet is probably the best spot, but as I move forward, an envelope hits the floor. My stomach drops as my name stares back at me. I already got my letter; he told me how much he loved my friendship. How I was the brother he never had and that I should always live life to the fullest. But this is something else, and if it was in this magazine, he'd wanted to make sure I was the only one who saw it.

I pick up the envelope, quickly stash the magazine, and sit on the end of his bed. I swear, if this letter tells me about a woman he knocked up or if there is a body decaying somewhere, I may bring him back to life just to kill him myself.

I blow out a breath and rip open the envelope, revealing the letter inside.

Hey man, I see you found my letter. I knew I could trust you to hide that magazine, but did you ogle the pictures first? Don't lie, we both know you did.

In my last letter, I told you all my sappy heartfelt crap, but in this one, I need to take a serious tone. I am going to be gone soon and there is something I need from you.

I need you to look after Julia. She needs an older brother to look after her, and if she marries Jacob, help her with anything she needs. If she doesn't marry him, make sure whoever she is with is worthy of her, and if he's a tool, send him packing in a way that would make me proud.

I laugh at his words as tears well up in my eyes. He felt the need to tell me to watch over his sister, but he never needed to. I have been here for all of them every day since he died and plan to be forever.

Now, we need to talk about Katie. She's going to take me leaving the hardest, and don't be surprised if she disappears for a bit. She has always tried to run away from pain rather than face it. Just don't let her run forever, don't give up on her. I know you're in love with her but stayed away for me. Well, Travis, if she's it for you, then go get her! Love her well, cherish her always, and make all her dreams come true. There is no one else I would rather entrust my sister's heart to. I see all the love you have for her.

And if I have to spell it out for you, let me tell you Katie loves you, too. So, don't be the idiot we both know you can be by letting her slip away.

I love you, brother. Take care of my girls. I'll see you on the other side.

—Jeff

My head is spinning. All this time he knew, for all this time I've had his blessing to be with her. I fold the letter and place it back into the envelope for safekeeping.

I have to find Katie.

I have to tell her that her brother knew.

Hope and excitement fill every fiber of me.

I dash from his room with both of our letters and take off toward the guesthouse, praying he was right and that she loves me, too.

I burst through the front door.

"Katie!" I yell.

The hope and joy in my chest are threatening to internally combust. I actually have a shot here, but she doesn't answer.

"Katie!" I yell again, jogging to her door and knocking on it. No answer. The bathroom is open, the kitchen is mostly clean, and the cookies are gone.

"Katie!" My tone has taken a turn toward desperation. I check my room just to be sure and then return to the kitchen.

I realize again that the cookies are gone, and it finally dawns on me what that means. My gut sinks. She's already left for the rehearsal.

CHAPTER 8

Katie

THE WEDDING REHEARSAL IS IN full swing at the country club, and Julia is practically vibrating with excitement. I stand next to her in the line of bridesmaids, but I'm admittedly distracted.

Travis looks impeccable as he stands next to Jacob in the line of groomsmen. He kept it simple this evening with a white, button-up, long-sleeve shirt, loosely tucked into a pair of khaki dress pants. Thankfully, we were not paired together to walk down the aisle before the bride. So, my plan of avoidance is working perfectly thus far, even though all my heart wants is to kiss him again, and my body craves to feel his strong arms hold me once more.

"All right!" Jules cheers. "That's a wrap on the

rehearsal, and dinner will be in the reception area. The rest of our families should be arriving soon and then we'll eat!" She clasps her hands together in front of her as she bounces on her toes with uncontained excitement.

"One last thing," Jacob continues. "I want to thank you all for being part of this special day." His eyes find mine and it's like he's speaking directly to me. "This day would not be the same without you here. Julia and I love and appreciate you all." He breaks eye contact with me after that. "Now, let's head to the reception area."

I have been so distant from my family for so long that his words feel like a gut punch. I'm not sure if I deserve the love and devotion that my sister and soon-to-be brother-in-law offer me so freely. For once, I find myself truly questioning if leaving home was ever the right thing to do. I pushed everyone away for the safety of *my* heart, but I never paid any attention to theirs. They all lost Jeff, too, and when I left, I took myself away. I wasn't there for any of them. I just did what I do best—I ran.

I spot Travis making his way through the rest of the bridal party and heading straight toward me. He looks determined, his jaw set and shoulders taut, yet there's a light in his eyes that wasn't there before. Apparently, he's not willing to forget about our kiss.

Hastily, I turn and move toward the women's restroom. (Have I mentioned that I'm really good at running away?) I won't be able to hide in here all night, but at least it will give me a moment to gather my thoughts, and with any luck, Travis will be pulled away by someone. Surely there are people here who just can't wait to hear all of the details he's willing to share about the bakery fire last night; they've probably been waiting for their chance to pounce.

I make it to the bathroom before Travis reaches me, and I lean against the wall, letting the weight fall from my shoulders.

Thankfully, no one else is in here now to see me in all my trainwreck glory.

My reprieve doesn't last long, though.

At the bathroom counter, I'm looking over my makeup when two of the other bridesmaids, and Jules's close friends, Marie and Amy, walk in. I never truly cared for these two but always put up with them for Jules. They're a bit too snobbish for my liking.

"Did you see Travis this evening?" Marie says, fanning herself like an idiot.

"Um, of course. Those khakis he's wearing complement his backside *real* well," Amy teasingly jeers right before drowning her lips in more of her pinkish-colored gloss.

Something dark coils itself in my gut at their words. Travis may never be mine, but over my dead body will he be either of theirs. He's more than a piece of meat. He is funny, playful, and so caring he would put anyone else's needs above his own always. All these two know is how to take and use.

"What I wouldn't give to tie that man down."

Marie smiles, and something in me snaps.

"Sorry to say it, girls, but Travis is gay." I cross my arms over my chest and lean my backside against the vanity.

"What?" They both eye me skeptically. "No way—he was the biggest player back in the day!" Amy rolls her eyes.

"No, really. He was just exploring back then. He's gay, and I would know since he was my brother's best friend and is still close with my family."

I do my best to stay casual, but worry coils in my gut. I should have come up with something better to say, but this was the first thing to pop into my mind.

"Ugh, whatever." Marie looks disappointed. "Why are the hottest ones always gay?"

"Well, either way. He's fine to look at," Amy jests to Marie. "You know my cousin Max is single. Maybe I can introduce them?"

I turn from them with a smile of victory on my face. I've been in here for a while now, so with any luck, Travis is gone.

When I emerge, I spot him in conversation with Jacob on the other side of the reception hall. Relief and a little bit of guilt wash over me. I am successfully avoiding him, but something happened in that bathroom that I'm not ready to face, and I just told the gossip queens of Lakes that he is undoubtedly gay.

Our eyes lock across the room, and I watch as he slaps Jacob on the back and heads my way.

Crap.

Why did I have to look over there? He probably wouldn't have even noticed me if I hadn't.

I move across the room to a slightly secluded corner, hoping to hide in the shadows, and that's when I witness Amy stop Travis in his tracks.

This night could not get any worse.

I see the moment she mentions something about him being gay, because his eyebrows raise in surprise and then he smirks and glances in my direction.

He politely excuses himself from their discussion and heads straight for me. If I wanted this man to forget all about me and move on with his life, I'm doing a horrible job.

Within moments, he's in front of me.

"I finally found you, Gummy Bear."

"What do you want, Travis? I need to check in with the caterer."

It's a load of bull.

And he knows it.

"We need to talk abo—"

"We have nothing to talk about. You kissed me and nothing more. Just let it go, and we can pretend it never happened. Now, I have things to attend to and then a cake to finish decorating. Please text me with details about how Jules wants it done." I say it all matter of fact–like, but I feel like I want to vomit as soon as the words leave my mouth.

I try to move past him, and he blocks me. His light demeanor shifts as his shoulders tense and his mouth presses into a flat line.

"Right, it meant nothing, and that's why you told Amy I'm gay."

My cheeks heat with the embarrassment of having been caught lying to keep them away from him.

I really should've come up with something better to say.

"They were just . . . they, um." I stumble over my words, but I can't come up with an excuse that doesn't give credit to the green monster living in my gut.

"Whatever, Katie. You know, if you could let go of the past and admit to yourself for just a second that we have something here, we may actually have a shot. I went to Jeff's room and got this for you."

He pulls an envelope from his back pocket and pushes it into my hand.

"He left us all letters, but you took off before we found them. Have a good evening."

He stalks away from me and leaves me in the corner, shellshocked.

My body begins to shake and tears well in my eyes. I no longer need to avoid Travis since I have successfully pushed him away, and now I must face something even more daunting.

I'm holding my brother's final words to me. Words I desperately crave and am absolutely terrified to read.

I grip the envelope to my chest and hastily retreat from the room to find somewhere to be alone.

Down the hall, I locate a lounge area that has a door I can shut behind me. I sit in a giant, overstuffed armchair and stare at the envelope in my hand. *Katie* is scribbled on the front in my brother's handwriting. Will he tell me he loves me one last time, tell me to chase after my dreams?

He was my rock, and now I have to face these feelings of loss all over again. Jeff always knew what I needed before I ever had a clue. He was always a shoulder to cry on, and a listening ear without judgment. He was the first to defend me, even when I was guilty. No matter what I faced, my brother had my back. To this day, my parents don't know I was actually the one who sneaked out and wrecked the old truck when I was sixteen. I called Jeff when it happened, and he took the blame for driving into the side of the neighbor's barn.

Now, every wall I've built to keep my grief at bay threatens to crumble to nothing.

Tears stream down my cheeks and my hands tremble as I slowly open the letter, completely unprepared for what his final words to me may say.

Hey there, Gummy Bear. If you're reading this then I am gone, and there are a few things I need you to know.

I pause and a sob pours out of me. Of course he would call me Gummy Bear in his goodbye letter. I throw my head back as the pain in my chest floods through me like a broken dam.

First, I need you to know how much I love you. Little sis, even beyond the grave I will be loving you. Something as small as death couldn't stop me from watching over you.

I laugh slightly. Only Jeff would imply death is a small inconvenience.

"I love you, too, big brother," I whisper in a broken voice.

Second, I know you well enough to know that you're going to hide. You would rather outrun the pain than face it, but Katie, that is no way to live your life. Me being gone will hurt forever, but I promise it will get easier over time.

It hasn't, though. His death hurts like the fresh wound it is.

As much as I try, I can never escape the reality that he's gone forever.

Lastly, and this is the most important, chase your dreams as a baker but don't forget to find love. I won't be there to see it, but I know you're in love with Travis. You promised me you would stay away from him, and that was the right call when we were young. But I know beyond a shadow of a doubt that he will grow up to be an honorable man, and that is when he will be ready for an amazing girl like you. Katie, he will protect you, support you, and provide for you till his dying breath if you'll have him. I can see it in the way he watches you and how he hangs on your every word. You've had his heart forever; he just needs time to grow into a man worthy of you. So, my sweet sister, go build a life with him, if that is what you want.

The only thing I want for you, little Gummy Bear, is to find happiness and to know how grateful I am that I got to be your big brother.

Love you always and forever,

—Jeff

My heart feels so full and so racked with grief that all I can do is stare at the letter as tears stream down my face. I cry until I feel so devoid of emotion that I slowly peel my trembling body from the chair and head back to my parents' house, leaving the party and Travis behind. I have a cake to decorate and maybe, just maybe, in that space I will find my next step.

CHAPTER 9

Travis

THE REST OF THE EVENING went by in a blur. I knew that letter would be hard for her, and a primal need to be with her has been gnawing at me ever since my frustration dissipated. She never came back to the reception hall, and I know she holed up somewhere just out of my reach to cry her eyes out.

I played my part of enthusiastic groomsman for the evening for Jacob and Julia, but as soon as I could get away, I searched that building high and low for Katie. Finally, when I ran out of places to look, I checked the parking lot, and the car she borrowed from her parents was gone.

I'm almost back to the guesthouse now, and anxiety is coursing through my veins with the fear that Jeff's letter might have sent her running to Michigan again, but this time, I will do what I should have done then. This time, I'll follow her. I'm done letting her run away.

From her feelings. From us. From me.

Relief fills me when I enter the guesthouse and her clutch is lying on the table and her shoes are by the door.

In the kitchen, I'm surprised to find that the cake is completely done. Covered in white fondant and topped with beautiful flowers of various shapes and colors. Katie sure did make a masterpiece this evening.

While knocking on her closed bedroom door, I brace myself for the possibility that she's angry with me, but there's no answer. I have to put my mind to rest, so I slowly push the door open to peek inside. She's asleep with her letter clutched to her chest like she can feel her brother's warmth through it.

I should have been there for her when she read that letter, but I can't focus on that. I need a plan to win this girl—and fast. Tomorrow is the wedding and what feels like the last chance I'll have to prove myself to the woman I've wanted to be with for years.

CHAPTER 10

Katie

THE MORNING HAS BEEN NOTHING but a flurry between the hair, the makeup, the dresses. It's all one chaotic work of art. Julia looks like an absolute princess in her flowing, white gown, hair in a braided bun, topped with a veil hairpiece.

"Are you ready for this?" I ask before opening the dressing room door to where my dad is waiting to walk her down the aisle.

She beams at me and is completely radiant. "I've never been more ready for anything in my whole life."

I nod, turning to the door.

"Katie."

I pause.

"When this is your day, you'll feel this too."

She smiles at me.

I chuckle and turn to fully face her. "Feel what?"

"This feeling that no amount of pain or fear will ever be able to cripple you because you have him. That the love you share is enough to conquer it all."

I pad at my lavender dress and hope blooms in my chest. Maybe someday I'll find a love like that. Maybe someday . . . that could be me and Travis.

I smile at her and kiss her cheek softly, before turning back to the door.

I open the door to my dad, dressed in a full suit, and he places a hand on his chest at the sight of us.

"My girls. You both look absolutely stunning," he gushes.

I step forward and hug him before moving out of the way so he can embrace Julia while I take my spot in the lineup next to one of the groomsmen.

The music begins to play and we walk down the aisle, taking our spots on either side of the preacher and Jacob.

The music changes, and Julia starts down the aisle with my dad gripping her tightly and holding back tears.

Jacob smiles at his bride like he is the happiest man on Earth, with nothing but love and devotion.

I know I should be focused solely on my sister today, but through the whole exchange of vows, my eyes are on Travis.

Jeff knew, and now I have his blessing, but is this what I want? To be with Travis?

I think … I think I really do. No man has ever pulled me in with such a gravitational force. He has insisted on being there for me, even as I shoved him away—and never even held a grudge. Jeff wasn't wrong about the man Travis grew into. I can trust him with my heart and know he won't ever break it. He can get under my skin like no one ever has, but because of that, he sees pieces of me that no one else can see. Travis Hardy, might just be it for me.

The crowd erupts with applause and pulls me from my thoughts.

"Now introducing Mr. and Mrs. Jacob White," the officiant declares, and I smile at my perfect sister. I'm so happy she got her happy ending.

The reception is in full swing, but I'm in nothing but a cloud. I want to talk to Travis, to tell him about the letter, to tell him I want to try this even though I have no idea how it will work.

"All right, folks, before we do the bride and groom's first dance, they have requested a dance in memory of Julia's older brother," the DJ says above the crowd's noise. "Can I please have Travis Hardy and Katie Nash on the dance floor for the Jeffrey Nash dance?"

My stomach sinks as my eyes find Julia and Jacob. They're grinning with excitement, and I have no idea why, because this wasn't on the itinerary.

On the dance floor, Travis takes my waist, and I place one hand on his shoulder and the other in his hand. The song "A Thousand Years" by Christina Perri drifts from the speakers as he begins leading me around the floor.

"Travis, what is this?" I look up at him, and my heart swells as his eyes meet mine.

"This is me shooting my shot, Gummy Bear."

He smiles at me softly, then dips me down and pulls me back closer to his chest.

"Katie, I've wanted to be with you since we were teenagers, but I wasn't ready for you. When you left for Michigan, a piece of me left with you, and I didn't truly realize it until that day I kissed you in the kitchen. Sweetheart, I want this, and I want you."

A small tear streaks down my cheek at his words. "How, Travis? I live in Michigan now. It can't work."

"Of course it can. I have nothing holding me here anymore. The bakery needs a decent number of repairs before it can open, so I'll have it fixed up before either selling or leasing it out. *You're* what matters to me. I can run a bakery anywhere, so I'll come to Michigan with you."

With that, I grab his face and kiss him. Pouring every ounce of my feelings into it. Letting the sparks fly through my body and savoring the feeling. Jeff had been right about all of it.

Julia and Jacob start cheering, and the crowd joins in. I pull away from Travis, but he folds me into his arms.

"Looks like more love is blossoming tonight. Let's hear it for Travis Hardy and Katie Nash!" the DJ says.

Travis looks to me with a longing in his eyes that I'm sure matches mine. "So, are we doing this, sweetheart?"

"Yeah, I think we are." I smile up at him. "But if you think catching me was the hard part, you have no idea how needy of a girlfriend I'll be," I tease.

"Oh, I plan to spoil you rotten, Gummy Bear." He chuckles and kisses me softly on the forehead. "You're mine now, and I'll let everything else crumble to pieces before I let you slip away again."

I am not sure what our future holds or what our life in Michigan will even look like, but it's time I stop running from things and start running toward them, starting with Travis Hardy.

CHAPTER 11

Travis

I CAN HONESTLY SAY LAST night was the best night of my life. If I hadn't woken to her snuggled next me in bed this morning, I may have thought it had all just been a perfect dream.

I look toward the sun-filled sky, soaking in the feel of the rays on my skin as I lean against my car door. Katie is at breakfast with her mom, canceling flights so we can drive back with my car instead. Her being there this morning gave me the perfect opportunity to come here before we leave this afternoon.

I push off my car door and walk the grassy path until I reach Jeff's black granite gravestone. This is where my best friend was laid to rest, and even though he has passed on, I still think he watches over all of us.

Kneeling down, I place my hand on top of the stone and my heart aches.

"Hey," I mutter looking at the ground. "So, you were right. I love Katie, and it turns out she loves me, too. I just wish you were here to see it. We all miss you so much, but I needed to come say goodbye. I'm following Katie back to Michigan, and I wanted to tell you that I'll take care of her as long as she lets me. Thank you, brother, for trusting me with your sister's heart even though I'm not sure I'll ever be worthy of it."

A wind blows through the graveyard, and a sense of peace fills my chest. He knows. That's the only feeling left inside my gut.

I nod to the grave and stand, stuffing away the ache inside. "I love you, brother, and I'll come see you when we come to visit."

I turn away from the stone and walk back to my car. My eyes will no longer seek moments from the past. I'll look only to the future, my future with *her*.

In one weekend, my entire life has changed. A fire put my business out of commission until repairs are done, Katie went from being a ghost of the past that held my heart to being the woman I get to call mine, and now I'm moving to Michigan. If this was always going to be the end result to Julia and Jacob's wedding weekend, I would have kicked their butts down the aisle years ago.

Once I'm back at my car, I make the short drive to

the bakery. The fire department said I could come grab some things from my apartment with an escort, but that most of what's there wasn't salvageable. I'm not sure I'm prepared to see it, but I'm also not sure when I'll be back.

I pull up to the back of the building and from here, it looks normal, like nothing happened at all. A brick sits in my gut knowing the damage that lay just behind the walls. I just hope the irreplaceable things are still intact. That will be a difficult pill to swallow if not.

Jacob is standing at the foot of the steps with his Fire Rescue shirt tucked into a pair of blue slacks, and I can only shake my head when he waves at me. He and Julia don't fly out for their Australian honeymoon until this evening, so I'm sure he insisted on being my escort.

I climb out and make my way to him as a sick feeling rolls through me. The air still smells of burnt wood and smoke. I don't want to do this, but the sooner I do, the sooner I can get back to my girl.

I'll never get over the blooming warmth the knowledge of her being mine brings me.

"Aren't you supposed to be wrapped up in some sheets or something with your new bride?" I ask as I near him.

"Ha ha, very funny. Jules went to breakfast with her mom, too, and I figured you could use a friend rather than just another firefighter today." He gives me a kind smile, and I clap a hand on his shoulder.

"Well, I appreciate it, man. Let's get this over with."

He nods, and I climb the steps and open the door, revealing the one-room studio apartment that I've called home for so long and immediately feeling like I've been punched in the gut.

Caution tape blocks access to the left side of my studio—my personal kitchen—which is charred and almost unrecognizable. I suck in a breath and step inside fully, examining the soot-covered walls and all of my possessions in that area, big and small, just . . . black. Melted. Gone.

"Chief Morgan told me not much was salvageable up here, but it's different seeing it in person," I mutter.

"Yeah, it's pretty rough, but the bed area was mostly untouched."

Jacob gestures to my sleeping area, and most everything is still intact. I walk over to my bed and nightstand, leaving Jacob lingering in the doorway. This is where the important things are.

The picture of Katie, Jeff, and me at the town carnival from high school sits atop the nightstand covered in soot but looks fine behind the glass surface. I move to pull open the drawer and inside is Jeff's letter, more pictures, and my documents like my birth certificate and such.

I empty the nightstand into a bag and grab the picture frame. These were the irreplaceable things, and by some miracle, they were untouched. I don't need to see anything else. I don't want to see anything else. I just want to get back to the woman I've waited years for.

"That's all?" Jacob eyebrows pinch and his face laces with concern. "We could go see the bakery kitchen if you want? The fire started in there from faulty wiring in the industrial fridge unit. We think it shorted out and threw some sparks from the wall socket—just enough to catch the boxes on the floor next to it."

I appreciate his friendship more than I think I've really ever expressed. "That sounds like something for the insurance company and the contractors to do. I've got what I need. Now I'm just ready to get back to Katie."

He nods and follows me out the door and down the steps. "So, what's the plan here now? It's all just moving really fast."

"I really appreciate you and Julia and everything, but I can't waste another minute. I've already lost five years, and I'm ready to run into a life with her, not take baby steps."

"I'm happy for you. Just stay safe, and take care of both of you," he says, and I smile at my friend and wrap my arms around his shoulders as we smack each other's backs in a hug.

"Text me when you're safe in the Mitten State, but don't call. I've got plans that involve bedsheets and my wife." He wags his eyebrows at me, and we both laugh.

"You two have a blast on your trip, and don't do anything I wouldn't," I tease as I head to my car.

"That's a pretty short list!" Jacob yells, and I laugh once more and turn to throw my hands out at my side in an unapologetic shrug.

Back at the house, Katie is sitting on the porch of the guesthouse with her luggage by the door. She is basking in the sun's rays, and she looks like an elegant piece of art. My chest ignites at the sight of her, and all the uneasy feelings clinging to me from what I'd seen at the bakery dissipate. I climb from my car, and she stands, gripping her luggage.

"Ready to hit the road, big guy?" she yells from the porch as I approach.

"I've never been more ready for anything."

I wrap my hands around her waist and crash my lips against hers. She wraps her arms around my neck and my hand laces through her soft hair.

I'll never get enough of this. I'll never get enough of her, and this is only the beginning.

I pull back and scoop her up into my arms, cradling her legs and her shoulders.

She giggles and squeals in my arms. "What in the world are you doing?"

"I told you I was going to spoil you, so I figured I'd carry my woman to the car."

She slaps my chest playfully and a sense of contentment

fills me. This is all I need right here. This sweet, happy, soft woman in my arms.

"You are absolutely ridiculous." She beams as I place her into the passenger seat of my car.

"Maybe, but you chose me, so you better get used to it."

She rolls her eyes, and I kiss her forehead before shutting the door.

I jog to the porch where her luggage is, and I spot Mr. and Mrs. Nash walking down the driveway toward us.

I grab Katie's things and place them in the trunk and then meet the people who have basically always been my second family.

"I know you weren't trying to sneak away without saying goodbye, right?" Mrs. Nash walks up to me and embraces me in a warm hug. Her hugs are the best; there's nothing like the comfort of a mother's hug.

"I wouldn't dream of it."

She pulls back and stares at me, adoration in her eyes.

"We said goodbye to Katie in the house, but I couldn't let you leave without a proper goodbye." Her eyes shine with tears, and she embraces me once more.

"Be safe and make sure to call." She releases me and steps back.

"I will, and we'll be back soon."

She smiles and dabs at her eyes with the sleeve of her shirt.

My chest pangs at the sight of her sadness. I didn't think it would be this hard to leave them—my parents didn't seem to have a hard time driving off in their RV—but I know that they're just as happy as I am that I'm going with Katie this time.

I turn to Mr. Nash next. He holds out his hand and I take it, sharing a firm handshake. "I'm going to miss seeing you around here."

"I'm going to miss all of you, too."

We release hands, and he slaps my shoulder.

"Take care of my girl." His sad smile threatens to break my heart in two.

"I will, and I promise to bring her back to you soon."

"I'll hold you to that, son." We both chuckle, though I know he's serious . . . but so am I. Katie stayed away far too long last time.

I step back and walk to the car, the vehicle that will take me into my new future. It's bittersweet leaving the life I've known behind, but with *her* by my side, my future is looking sweeter than pie.

I climb into the driver's seat and start the car. Katie sets her phone down and stares at me.

"You're sure you want this? You want to come to Michigan? We could try the long-distance thing—"

"Gummy Bear, I've never been more certain of a decision in my life."

I turn to look into her beautiful eyes.

"You're it for me. You've always been it for me, and

I'm not going to waste another moment without you by my side."

She grabs my face in both her hands and kisses me deeply. "Let's go then."

I nod at her and put the car into reverse. We wave to her parents as we pull out the long driveway, and I envelope her hand in mine. For the first time in years, I finally feel whole, and I know that as long as I have her by my side, I will always be right where I need to be.

EPILOGUE

Katie

"KATIE, YOUR SISTER'S CALLING." TRAVIS shakes my phone at me from the living room couch, and I abandon the cookie dough I was working on to go get it.

These past four months have been nothing short of perfect. Travis has made this tiny shell of an apartment feel like a home. I still support everything with my freelance work, while Travis has been sorting out the bakery back home.

It's been a rough process, but the last of the repairs will be done this week and then we will decide what to do with it from there.

I grab the phone from his hand and kiss him on the cheek before plopping down in the armchair to answer it.

"Hey Jules, what's up?"

"Hey! Jacob's here, too," she squeals. "Is Travis with you?"

"Yeah, why?" I ask as my eyebrows furrow and a nervous energy fills me.

Jules and I make a habit of talking almost every other day since she got back from Australia and never once has she asked me if Travis was nearby. Something's up.

"Put us on speakerphone!" she demands.

I climb from the chair and crawl into Travis's lap. He tucks me into his arms, and I place the phone on my lap and hit the speaker button.

"Okay, we're both here now." My voice is laced with apprehension, and Travis rubs my arms, providing me with a silent comfort.

"WE'RE PREGNANT!" Jacob and Jules shout in unison, and my jaw almost hits the floor.

"Holy crap! A baby!" I shout back in excitement.

"Congratulations, you guys!" Travis shouts and kisses my cheek. "Do I get to call you Aunt Gummy Bear now?" He teases me quietly. I smack his chest.

"We just found out, but I had to call you first. We're doing a big reveal for Mom and Dad this weekend."

My gut clenches slightly knowing I'll miss that.

"This is amazing news, Jules," I gush. "Will you record Mom and Dad for me?"

"Well, duh, and thank you! I have to go and call Jacob's brother now! Love you!"

"Okay. Love you! Bye!" I shout as she ends the call.

I turn to Travis and nuzzle my face into his chest. My sister is going to be a mom. I can't believe it. I'm going to be an aunt.

I pull back from Travis and look at him. His soft smile warms my chest, but . . . I hate that we're here and everything is back there. I wasn't there for her after Jeff died. I wasn't there for her during her engagement. I want to be there for her now.

"Oh boy," Travis groans. "I know that look. What's going through that pretty little head of yours?"

"I'm just thinking about home, the baby, how to support my sister." I shake my head at my own words.

"You can be a great aunt and sister, even from Michigan. We already have a trip planned to go back next month." He rubs my arms soothingly.

"I know I can." I pause to let my next statement solidify in my mind before speaking. "But what if I don't want to?"

I meet his eyes and confusion etches his features.

"Are you suggesting moving back to Lakes?"

I nod as I bite my bottom lip nervously. Being here in Michigan is nice, but *Travis* is what makes it nice. I have no need or real desire to be here anymore. I had to face my pain of losing Jeff and it still hurts, but in that I now know I can't abandon those I love anymore.

"You're sure this is what you want?" he asks, trying to read my face.

"Yes. I want to move into your newly renovated apartment. We can open the bakery back up and run it together and maybe build a family of our own someday."

Travis cups my cheek and presses his lips to mine, his kiss deep and full of love. I melt into him the same way I did the first time we kissed in the guesthouse kitchen. My body molds into his, and I savor every vibrant touch of skin. His hand cups my cheek and brushes my hair back, and my skin ignites with beautiful prickles. I hope those never leave. . . .

He pulls back, and I rest my forehead against his.

"I guess we're moving next month instead of just visiting. Sweetheart, you better get packing."

I smile and bite my bottom lip while lacing my fingers through his long hair.

"And as far as the family part goes, I'll marry you tomorrow and have you pregnant by next week if that's what you want."

"How about we move first," I tease, and he scoops me up into his arms, cradling me.

Julia was right the day she got married. No pain or fear can ever cripple me again. Not with Travis holding my heart. My brother's best friend has become my forever.

About the Author

J.E. Smith is a romance enthusiast who loves to write sassy heroines and book boyfriends that make you swoon. Her short story "Cows & Kisses" was featured in *As the Snow Drifts: A Cozy Winter Anthology*, published by And You Press in 2024, and was released with an additional chapter by Attic Ebooks in 2025.

Author photo by Alesha Schultz-Hams

She resides in a small town outside of Grand Rapids, Michigan, where she enjoys country life with her family.

When she is not writing or lost in a new book, she loves to travel and explore the beauties of nature.

You can find Smith on Instagram
@author_j.e.smith

Acknowledgments

Here we are again with another wonderful story! I still can't believe I get to sit and write an acknowledgment page for another publication! To say I feel blessed and honored is an understatement!

This story has been a wonderful journey from the original story in the *Recipes for Romance* anthology to having it as its own novella. I will forever be grateful to my publisher, Nicole Frail, for giving me a shot with my first story and continuing to stick with me! Every story we do together, you help me grow as an author. Thank you!

Outside of the publishing realm, I want to give a shout-out to my amazing mother. You have been an amazing cheerleader, sounding board, and last-minute babysitter! I wouldn't be here right now without you!

Finally, thank you to my readers! You are the ones who make the actual dream come true! You reading my stories is what breathes life into this author's bones! I hope you loved reading *Baked In Love* as much as I loved writing it.

Also Available

Cows & Kisses

Best friends Ben and Maggie grew up together on neigh-boring ranches, and now they both help Maggie's father run the family farm.

As a winter storm approaches, the pair set out to bring in the cows, but what was supposed to be a one-day journey takes longer than expected and forces them to set up camp overnight.

And they only have one tent.

Available as an ebook.
Ebook ISBN: 978-1-965852-22-4

As the Snow Drifts

Don your cozy socks, snuggle under your favorite fuzzy blanket, grab your tea (or hot chocolate!), and get ready to settle in with a collection of short fiction that will transport you from the blistering cold of the midwestern prairies and farmlands to the warmth of festive B&Bs and coffee shops while the snow falls gently outside.

Available in paperback & ebook.
Paperback ISBN: 978-1-965852-02-6
Ebook ISBN: 978-1-965852-01-9

Recipes for Romance

The characters in this wholesome short story collection are open to finding love, showing love, and rekindling long-lost love while cooking, baking, snacking, and sipping their way through dates, heartaches, memories, and personal triumphs. These sweet stories will leave you feeling good. And maybe a little hungry.

Available in paperback & ebook.
Paperback ISBN: 978-1-965852-12-5
Ebook ISBN: 978-1-965852-11-8

Attic Books and Attic Ebooks
are imprints of Nicole Frail Books, LLC,
an independent ("indie") publishing
company located in Avoca, Pennsylvania.

Attic Ebooks is a digital-first imprint and is
open to submissions of various lengths,
including short stories and essays and
novellas. If the length and market allows,
longer works are considered for print with
Attic Books.

To learn more about submitting a query to
Attic Ebook, visit www.attic-ebooks.com.

Readers!
Join the NFB Street Team for exclusive first
reads and swag from Attic & Attic Ebooks!
www.nicolefrailbooks.com/street